For the scurvy Capsticks, who dared to
holiday with PIRATES!

And . . .
For Tamlyn, Lisa, Mike, and Cursed Katie,
who were press-ganged on a voyage that
they thought would never end . . .

First U.S. edition 2018

Library of Congress Catalog Card Number pending
ISBN 978-0-7636-9293-3

18 19 20 21 22 23 LEO 10 9 8 7 6 5 4 3 2 1

Printed in Heshan, Guangdong, China

This book was typeset in Aunt Mildred and Tree Persimmon.
The illustrations were sketched
with pencil and colored digitally.

TEMPLAR BOOKS
an imprint of
Candlewick Press
99 Dover Street
Somerville, Massachusetts 02144
www.candlewick.com

The Pirates of Scurvy Sands

Starring THE JOLLEY-ROGERS

JONNY DUDDLE

ⓣ

templar books
an imprint of Candlewick Press

Matilda lived in Dull-on-Sea, a charming seaside town—bleak all through the winter . .

but in summer, folks came down. They frolicked in the sea and played in the arcades; they sizzled in the midday sun and dug with plastic spades.

Matilda had a pen pal
who sailed the scurvy sea:
a pirate boy named Jim Lad.
He sent letters frequently.

They came in old green bottles
that she fished up on her line.
Jim didn't have a phone,
but his notes would do just fine.

Dear Tilda,

We're goin' on a voyage, a special pirate trip!
We'll pick you up tomorrow, if ye can board our ship!
We're on our way to Dull-on-Sea, sailing through the night.
I'll see you shortly after dawn,
          by the early morning light.

          From,   Jim Lad

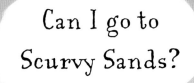

Can I go to Scurvy Sands?

Matilda asked her dad.

Oh ... Erm ...
I suppose you could.
Those pirates aren't
so bad.

Matilda packed her swimsuit,
some shorts and summer tops,
her toothbrush, snorkel, sunblock,
and her new flip-flops.

At dawn, Matilda's parents took her to the harborside, past the yachts to where the Jolley-Rogers' ship was tied.

ARR! Matilda!

Jim Lad yelled, swinging on a rope.

He landed—THUD—beside her and said:

Shall we elope?

They skimmed across the ocean, three days beneath the sails.

They sang sea shanties, played I Spy, and made up pirate tales.

My name is Cap'n Ollie Day! I hope ye'll all have fun! Make sure to slap yer lotion on before goin' in the sun!

Ride on the big dipper! Play upon the sand! Ye can shop for a new hook, if ye've lost yer hand!

Welcome to SCURVY SANDS!

If ye like to dig, ye could search for Mad Jack's gold! Buried deep beneath the sand since the days of old!

We've been diggin' here for years and years, but none who've looked have found the treasure that Mad Jack McMuddle dropped into the ground.

Here's your scurvy chalet. It's made from broken ships. There's a good view of the ocean and a whiff of fish and chips!
Tomorrow morning's Cruncher Club, so bring yer pirate kids! There'll be grub and shanties after dark, and wrestlin' with squids.
They call me Ratface Rodney. I wear a crimson jacket. If ye need a helping hook, just wave and make a racket!

The Jolley-Rogers
dropped their bags, and
Jim's mom made some tea.

What a lovely view,
and just a ship's length
from the sea!

The next day Jim and Tilda
went to Cruncher Club,
but amongst the other pirate kids
there was a big hubbub.

"I don't think she's a pirate,"

Cursed Katie mumbled. The others all agreed with her, shook their heads, and grumbled:

"That girl can't read a compass!"

"She don't know east from west!"

"She don't know port from starboard!"

"She won't pass the pirate test!"

THE PIRATE TEST
Name . . . .

Barnacle Bob, the lifeguard,
sat up and rubbed his eyes.
He thought he'd seen a lubber,
much to his surprise.

but maybe it's a
mermaid. With this
spyglass I can't see.

I'm sure
I see one swimmin'
in the scurvy sea . . .

Can she wield a cutlass?
Is she good at digging?
Can she shout "OOO-ARR!" as she's swinging from the rigging?

Philippa McCavity was shocked by what she saw.
She was blinded by the sparkles as
Matilda passed her door.

PRIVATEER DENTIST

BEFORE

AFTER

Her teeth are clean. This will not do. I'd really like to pull a few!

I'll feed her gum and lollipops, and all the sweets I've got.

I'll hide her pesky toothbrush, then I'm sure her teeth will rot!

Old Man Grumps looked anxious
as he plucked hairs from his beard.

My monkey can't
find any lice,
but says her hair
smells very nice!

I ain't seen
nothin' like it.
That little girl
is weird!

I'll mucky up her
gleamin' nails!
My scurvy nail bar
never fails!

Jim's dad's tummy rumbled.
"I need to get some grub.
My stomach's feeling peckish.
Let's eat at this here pub!"

Do you want some hard tack? Shark brains? Pickled eggs?

Seagull soup? Dodo burgers? Battered parrot legs?

THE WONKY COMPASS

Matilda turned a little green and ordered the grilled fish, with weevil-flavored mashed potatoes, served on a clean dish.

At a nearby table, Betty Bilge was not impressed.

Have ye seen how neatly that little girl is dressed?

She don't like maggot-y cookies!

Or shark brains steeped in brine!

The girl's a fussy eater! She don't act a bit like mine!

She's a bad example, with her knife and fork. If mine learn table manners, all my pirate friends will talk.

I don't think she's a pirate. She's clean and too polite. Since this place ain't for lubbers, it really isn't right!

Cap'n Day called the Jolley-Rogers to reception.

I've had complaints, but as ye know, it's all about perception.

We know that she's no pirate. And I'm afraid it just won't do—bringin' lubbers to Scurvy Sands. She ain't part of our crew!

Can she at least do pirate stuff to put their minds at rest?

Dig for treasure!

Fire a cannon!

Take the pirate test!

"The treasure!" Tilda whispered. "This portrait holds a clue."

We'll need a compass and Jack's map. I know what we should do!

I know my east from west, I do, but *Jack McMuddle* never knew his left from right or east from west!

HE didn't pass the pirate test!

Reading Mad Jack's map,
Matilda walked ahead.
Jim Lad marched along behind,
listening as she said:

To the west
of Scurvy Sands
sank my ship with
all its hands.

I dragged my treasure chests ashore, where they shall lie forevermore.

"Why we headin' east?" said Jim. "When Mad Jack's map says west?"

"That's just it," Matilda said. "Jack FAILED the pirate test! Using his mirror to check his tattoo, he always had a backward view!"

I climbed along the jagged rocks, took off my coat, my shoes and socks.
To drag the chest took all my strength, but drag I did, a full ship's length!
?

m ran to join Matilda.

Is the treasure near?

X marks the spot!

Matilda said . . .

We need to dig RIGHT HERE!

Matilda's got such pretty hair!
I love her sparkly nails!
I'm such a lubber fan, y'know!
I'll miss her when she sails.
SQUEAK!

Thank you for my pirate trip. I've memories I'll treasure!

Anytime, Matilda. It was a scurvy pleasure!

The pirates wailed and waved good-bye.

Oh, I cannot help but cry!

They fired their cannons,
flintlocks, too,
and watched the *Matilda*
fade from view.

Though Matilda had a lot of fun,
she didn't mind the trip was done.
She really couldn't wait to be
landlubbing back in Dull-on-Sea!

To the EAST of Scurvy Sands sank me ship with all its hands. I dragged me treasure chests ashore, where they shall lie forevermore!

MAD JACK McMUDDLE

He always got lost and was never quite sure of which oceans he crossed. Since his map-reading skills went often awry, he'd a compass tattooed above his left eye.

Rats in yer bilges? King chopped off yer hand? Treasure lost its sparkle?

Then come to
SCURVY SANDS!

PARK yer SHIP in HERE

Mad Jack's Water Park

Paddle Boats